YELLOW EYES IN THE GARDEN

Other books by Douglas Atwill
from
Boxwood Press

Douglas Atwill Houses, 2016
Bonfire, 2017

All books available in Santa Fe, NM at

COLLECTED WORKS BOOKSTORE
202 Galisteo Street, 87501

OP. CIT. BOOKS
157 Paseo de Peralta, 87501

GARCIA STREET BOOKS
376 Garcia Street, 87501

YELLOW
EYES
IN THE
GARDEN

FOUR STORIES

DOUGLAS ATWILL

BOXWOOD PRESS

Library of Congress Cataloging-in-Publication Data

Atwill, Douglas, author.
Yellow Eyes in the Garden: Four Stories / by Douglas Atwill.
ISBN: 1548663298
ISBN-13: 978-1548663292
Library of Congress Control Number: 2017911189

1. Short stories

Boxwood Press
PO Box 5959 Santa Fe NM 87502

CreateSpace Independent Publishing Platform, North Charleston, SC

ACKNOWLEDGEMENTS

These four stories were written over the last year, 2016, mostly in the afternoon, after a morning at the easel in the studio. Writing and painting are the two parts of my life now, with little else besides an episode of pruning the apple trees or pulling up a bunch of carrots in the vegetable garden. All these activities seem to meld together in my mind, one giving with grace into another. When the stories are nearly finished, I am lucky to have Wendy Schiller to edit them. She sees errors and ambiguity where I see none, and we only disagree on my use of the Oxford comma. Walter Cooper, Doug Bland, and Shelley McGehee are invaluable first readers. Billy Halsted and Wayne Bladh sit patiently still while I read the stories aloud. When the time seems right, I call Kathleen Dexter to put it all together into a book.

Thanks to all of them.

HEAVENLY BLOOMS

The abbey property, in the west country, far away from the growing sprawl of the urban areas, was sold during the years when the church needed cash. The expenses for the upkeep on this little-used abbey far exceeded the income it produced. It was thought that nobody would miss the rambling stone structure, almost a castle, and its surrounding acres, so far from the seat of power. Now that our beloved Abbot Sebastian had died, his good friend from seminary days, the archbishop, decided to lift this burden from the church. Converting such an unprofitable asset into money would make the archbishop and his circle more comfortable, yielding enough to replace their chamber draperies, buy a new Daimler for diocesan outings and, of course, deposit what might be left over into the Perpetual Fund. In time we brothers of St. Giles, trained to bend to the will of those on high, would be reassigned to the houses in Africa and South America that needed us. I sensed a disregard for the age and frailty of our band, brothers who had a certain stout spirit but very little in the way of physical strength.

A bishop, thin-lipped and pious, came from the city to deconsecrate the structure before the auction. Only we few Benedictine monks still in residence were the audience for this sad ritual, with its staccato Latin phrases and billows of green incense from Rome wafting upwards. The bishop took the vermeil and garnet candlesticks, the gold-washed offertory plates, and other ornaments with him in his two-door black coupe. He said he was returning these tokens of little value to the motherhouse in southern

France, but I wondered if they might be sitting in a lighted shop window in the city.

During the auction, a farmer named Roger Dockery put in the high bid for the abbey. He was not a devout man but a kind one nonetheless. He visited the abbey to try out the keys the day after the auction, his large hands tanned from the sun. As I watched him testing the main door, he asked, "Brother Michael, will you and the others stay on as custodians?"

"We cannot, Mister Dockery. The church has written that we will be reassigned in a month or two."

"That is so sad. But if you decide to stay on, I will pay you an ample amount quarterly to keep up the abbey property, just as you have been doing all these years."

"Thank you, but we are compelled to say no."

"I'll keep the offer open."

At forty, I was the youngest of the seven former monks, the rest being between seventy and eighty-five. We discussed the future that night, how our small group might have an alternative to being sent away for these remaining years. I related what Farmer Dockery had offered, in fact a place for us all to be safe for the rest of our lives. Discussion and consensus are not a natural exercise for monks, so I knew it was up to me to lead them. The Vatican, as if by omen, had recently shortened the process for leaving holy orders, which would now take many months instead of years. I knew in my heart it would be better for us to stay on, unfrocked, in the mossy courtyards of St. Giles than to be sent away.

"I will see to all the paperwork," I told them, "releasing us from our vows with honor. I cannot think of our beloved Brother Steven dusting fire-ants from the pews in the Upper Congo or any of us struggling to breathe in the thin air of Bolivia. We will live out our years, unfrocked, here at St. Giles."

Farmer Dockery came with a letter for us all to sign. In return for his payment, we would maintain the abbey, keep the doors working, repair windows, see that roofs do not leak – all of which we had been doing for decades. Dockery's sheep and cattle were already nibbling right up to the abbey foundations.

"And, sir, may we keep the produce from the abbey gardens?" I asked. "Vegetables are a large part of our diet."

"Of course. I want only the fields for my sheep and cattle."

His payment would not be sufficient for our annual upkeep; something more would be needed. I wondered if a solution would present itself.

Directly to the west were many acres of the abbey's virgin woodland, great oaks from medieval times and beech circles that must have seen pagan dances. In past years when I found a few hours free, I had explored the depths of the forest, once emerging several miles away. Dockery well knew the current high prices for hardwood flooring and furniture made from these fine native woods.

He also was aware that the grand stone buildings, courtyards, and walk-arounds had true value in themselves, apart from their spiritual tincture. It would be folly to allow them to crumble like so many other abbeys in the west country. Thus our symbiosis began – by safeguarding our home, we could stay on as maintenance men, while his sheep and cattle ate the formerly holy grasses. In time, he would harvest the oaks and elms, but we would have a home for the rest of our lives within the stone walls.

People have always given me responsibility, which even as an earnest choirboy I had accepted, agreeing to maintain the pitch for the organ, wax the choir-stalls, polish the altar brasses, organize the disarray on the library shelves or undertake whatever task was presented. Ultimately, as private secretary to the old abbot, I assumed all the accounting and correspondence duties as his disinterest in these tasks increased. In the end, there were more nursery and seed catalogs on his desk than churchly bulletins.

After the sale of the abbey, the older monks appointed me citizen-abbot to look after them and their interests. Most ex-clerics would be inclined to do that, a more natural choice for them than the confusing, democratic alternative. Of course, I stepped right into the role. It was in no way an official title or office, but I smiled every time they called me Abbot Michael. The trust of these men, bewildered at their future, pleased me. The reverse side of that coin, which filled my night thoughts, was that I was totally responsible for the well-being of six innocent men more like children than adults. The years behind abbey walls had erased their knowledge and natural distrust of the ways of the world. They did not want to think about their soon-to-be-lost vows, so I handled the endless paperwork and meetings which the laicizings entailed.

I loved Latin throughout my school years and often won awards and ribbons for my speeches, which I accompanied with hand gestures and expletives, often while wearing a toga. Odd as this was for a young student, I was also different from my classmates in other ways. Therefore, the choice to become a celibate monk came as a matter of course, even with the questions I had about faith. None of the other monks was interested in Latin more than as a part of the weekly service, but I kept up my fluency by reading on winter nights. The abbey library had leather-bound volumes of *The Gallic Wars*, *Tacitus*, *Orations of Cicero*, and *Letters of Pliny*. Abbot Sebastian often asked me to read aloud from these in his chamber, saying it was only a minor sin that he so relished my Latin pronunciations, especially the pluperfect verbs, an assertion to which I had no response.

I do not think that the city bishop who deconsecrated our abbey understood the odd parts of that rarely performed ritual, the ones in Latin that summoned evil wood-sprites, green men, and faeries to return from their primeval woods. As he peered through his half-glasses, tripping over the words *silvester malum*, *viridius*, and *diaboli minor*, my ears pricked up and I could not resist a smirk. He saw me and puffed a cloud of viridian incense my way, as if to quell my insolence. The abbey grounds would now be fair game for these creatures from the deepest forest. The holy circle was gone.

The gradual decline of the abbey gardens had accelerated during the last years of Abbot Sebastian. He was a sweet and holy man, but not the sort to run a difficult organization. Among my duties was the care of the vegetable garden. Since cabbages and turnips needed to flourish lest the whole abbey run hungry, I was excused from the matins and the compline and asked to attend vespers only when my work afforded time. Feeding my spirituality in the rows of carrots, I seldom attended.

The old abbot had strictly forbidden me to tend the other gardens, the flowering trees and shrubs which he

knew I loved. Vegetables and fruits for the tables were to be my priority, not the ornamental and colorful. Those flowering plants would not die for lack of care, because the mild, wet climate of the west country was a boon to plants, as he knew. However, I ceased the necessary pruning of the rare Levantine shrubs with their large bell-shaped flowers and the tying up of the fussy Bourbon roses. I knew that if we all did not obey our abbot, the whole tapestry of the abbey would unravel.

Prayer came hard for me. I always doubted that there was an ear up there listening. Brother Roland seemed to understand my predicament and told me that he would say all the prayers twice, once for himself, once for me. This just increased my feelings of being an outsider.

At the turn of the last century the abbey grounds displayed a collection of flowering shrubs, gardens with rare viburnums and camellias, species lilacs sent from church properties across the world. Immoderate abbey gardens, blooming and fragrant, were but a small part of the glory of God. If the faithful saw abundance and well-being surrounding the sacred stone structure, just as there were rich fabrics, polished silver, and brass inside, then there surely existed a similar perfection and abundance in heaven. Baskets of leafy vegetables, edible roots, corn, apples, quinces, pears, plums, Chinese peaches, and persimmons arrived in the kitchen, but one by one the ornamental borders grew wild and disorganized.

Lest I sound too proud of my gardening efforts, it must be said that the black earth of the abbey, a long-ago alluvium deposit, was rich and fertile. A band of very deep soil ran right across the west country, and the abbey had been sited in its very middle not by sheer chance.

Only small corrections to soil chemistry were needed to ensure success, season after season.

The oaken library of Abbot Sebastian is now my office, and I make a point of leaving the door open at all times. I asked the other brothers to come by at least once a week. Brother William had an interesting suggestion, one that I should have come up with myself.

"There are many seedlings around the magnolias. Could we pot them up and sell them?" he asked.

"A grand idea," I responded. "Some are very rare."

"I believe they have crossed with others, and the seedlings are new hybrids."

"Will you pot them all up, Brother William?"

"Of course. There are other shrubs that we could layer to cultivate young plants. Viburnums, old roses, azalea, camellias, and several others."

"You have a good eye, Brother William. I will help when I can."

"My family had a nursery in Shrewsbury."

This was the start of the Abbey Nursery. The years of neglectful gardening, allowing the seedlings to grow up willy-nilly, proved to be our salvation. Among the magnolias, we had thirty different varieties. Yellow magnolias from the Yunan hills, large pink magnolias from farther south, and a wonderful variant of the evergreen Carolina magnolia, with a white blossom and a broad yellow stripe. And who knew what delights awaited from the crossings that Brother William discovered?

We constructed a selling yard in the old meditation garden and I wrote a detailed sixty-page catalog, *Exotic Plants from the Abbey*. Brother William came up with the subtitle, *Heavenly Blooms*, which afforded us all a good laugh. Brother Edwin, the oldest of our group, made a detailed ink drawing of each offering, sometimes showing the root structure below. The village printer picked up our manuscript and converted it into a black and white printed catalog, placing all my Latin names in Caslon italic. I mailed a copy to every country house in the surrounding area and posted one in all the village pubs and post offices.

By the end of the first year, we had sold hundreds of pots from the yard and shipped as many more around the country in handmade beechwood boxes cushioned with moss. Word got back that customers treasured the boxes almost as much as the rare plants, and some brought them into the house to store their valuables. The imprimatur of an abbey on the nursery gave the suggestion, whatever it was truly worth, of an ethereal guarantee on the hardiness of the offerings.

It became obvious that we seven would survive against the strong winds of the outside world, prizing our self-worth with a growing assuredness. I set up an account with the local bank, depositing money at the end of every week. The Abbey Nursery was thriving. A discordant note was felt by all when our papers of laicization arrived from Rome, each with a circle of sealing wax and a florid official signature. I held on to the hope that the brothers' delight in their new nursery would eventually replace some of their quite different loss.

In the third year, a particular magnolia plant caught our attention. It had started as an ordinary seedling, but its ashen gray trunk grew higher than its siblings, and it was twice their height at the end of the year. We left it in place rather than potting it for sale. The next year it doubled

in height again, and in the next it branched out well over our heads. Its size alone was not what we marveled at – it produced the first bloom of that year, with enormous pale yellow blossoms. The petals curled upon themselves not unlike a Japanese peony, but twice the size. The inside filaments were of a deep gold and the blossoms sat upon the tree to exactly match the horizon, as in a Chinese print. It was the most vigorous and beautiful plant we had ever seen, and even its scent an ecstasy. Brother William named it for the father of the sun, Hyperion. We knew that magnolias combined both genders in one tree, but also knew without question that Hyperion was bursting with maleness. I could not help bragging a bit about him in our revised catalog of that year. To tease readers I wrote that the Magnolia Hyperion was not yet for sale, but could be viewed in early May. I designed a baluster fence to shield him from people getting too close, and we transplanted the siblings away, so the plant dominated the former meditation courtyard.

Visitors took me up on the offer, a crowd appearing every day in the first week of May. At night I wondered if it was wrong to exploit this innocent plant for our own uses, but knew that such beauty had to be shared with the world. By leaf-fall in the autumn, he had become a substantial young tree.

I had read about hybrid vigor in the old abbot's magazines, a condition that imparts to a plant an extraordinary ability to grow and bloom. A plant with such vigor springs high above the others, stronger and more vital. Sadly, nobody knew how to ensure that a new cross would have such vitality and only seldom did it occur.

In the next year during the weeks before our magnolia came into bloom, we had a visitor from the archdiocese in the city. He was a bishop who wanted to see our fabled plant while it was in its dormancy, to study the branches and bark for a report to the archbishop. Word had spread.

"Hasn't the Lord smiled on the abbey?" he asked, gracefully wending his way along to view the tree.

"Remember Your Excellence, it is no longer an official abbey," I said.

"Quite so. But it was when the tree was conceived."

"I am not so sure."

"This must be the correct time to transplant, before the leaves come out. The abbey tree should grace our more important garden in the city, where the archbishop and his monseigneurs can see it in their daily meditations, to glorify the church."

"We believe Magnolia Hyperion belongs here, where he was born."

"Then I will have the archbishop send a stern order for the transport of Magnolia Hyperion. What a blasphemous name! We will search scripture for one more suitable."

"But, sire, we are no longer monks and therefore no longer obliged to obey."

I was vexing our illustrious visitor, I knew, and this caused him to rearrange his cloak, flicking me a glimpse of its scarlet lining. I instinctively placed my feet wider apart, as if preparing for a physical blow from this old cleric.

"The archdiocese has talented and cunning solicitors," he said. "You can expect a strongly worded secular demand. Ancient agrarian rights and the like."

"Brother William will show you the way out."

"This will not end well, Abbot Michael."

It amused me to hear him address me that way, as if the title would encourage me to comply with his wish. Our magnolia would need protection, so the brothers kept watch over it each night in the old meditation gardens. Spring came and my desk was covered with letters from nurseries, asking for a viewing when the tree was fully in bloom. I was already sorry for the braggadocio in the latest catalog. The first of May arrived again and the tree presented dozens of yellow blossoms as large as dinner plates.

The nurserymen were an interesting lot, looking with envious eyes upon our darling. They whispered among themselves, clandestinely photographing the blossoms. We watched closely so as not to let them get inside the balusters, near enough to make a surreptitious cutting with a sharp knife. I had earlier asked the brothers to move the balusters farther out so there was no chance of anyone brushing against the tree. It brought me a coursing anger behind my ears even to think about so many hands caressing his smooth bark.

One nurseryman presented us with a written offer. He would pay four thousand pounds for all rights. Many more proposals followed, the highest more than three times the first offer.

We brothers met in my office. Brother William said that if we reproduced rooted cuttings for sale, it would take twelve years to sell enough of Hyperion to match the lowest offer. He had calculated that the highest offer was enough for us all to live on in the old abbey buildings for the rest of our lives. We would no longer be dependent on Farmer Dockery. The night ended with no decision, but I asked the brothers to request an answer at vespers.

I walked into the moonlit meditation garden and looked up at our son, thinking how odd it was that a group of celibate brothers had spawned such a handsome prince. What would be the consequences of selling him like a yearling bull, to be forcibly reproduced in the sooty nursery towns of the Midlands? I hoped the brothers would come to the decision that our son must stay here and that his offspring would not grace the many cottage gardens across the land, allowing small lads to jump up and pluck the celestial blooms every spring.

I should have known the brothers would agree with me. We locked the gates to the meditation garden, turning away the summer visitors who kept wanting to view what some were calling The Miracle Tree. Attractive as our nursery rows were with other seedlings and plants, everybody wanted those meditation garden doors to open again. We resisted.

It was a snowy winter and we brothers retreated to the few rooms that could be kept warm. We talked about what to do with our Magnolia Hyperion. The archbishop would not give up, we were sure. And the nurserymen, at least the unethical among them, might attempt to force an entry and dig up our tree. Either group might enlist the services of the local sheriff, who we knew could be bribed. It would be a dangerous spring if we did not come up with a solution while the snow was still on the ground.

The adjoining woodland provided us with the answer. I remembered a glade on the far side, an opening in the woods with a small field of grasses and wildflowers. If Hyperion were transplanted on the verge, he would thrive in the available sunlight, tended only with the native rain, like the other trees. We would see he got extra water and care in the early years. He would be safe from our archbishop or the nurserymen, and in another year he would be almost too big to transplant.

After a stretch of sunny winter days, the time had come. It was a difficult move. We covered his substantial root-ball with moist fabric and, all seven of us lifting, hoisted him horizontally on the cart used for bringing in hay bales. I thought of a wounded Greek warrior being carried home on his shield. I led the way to the glade and we planted him on a south-facing stretch of conifers, the older trees serving as a break from the harsh winter winds. We were all exhausted that night, but happy.

A few days later the city bishop, his driver and attendant standing behind him, knocked again on our doors. He was now in a heavier woolen winter cape, again lined with scarlet.

"The archbishop asks once more. If you cannot obey, we ask that you listen to the high angels and present the abbey magnolia to His Eminence," he said.

"We cannot, Excellency. Hyperion no longer lives in our meditation garden."

"Where, then?"

"In a better place."

"Have you killed it in a fit of ungodly spite?"

"We have given him a new, eternally sunny home."

"You have cut it down, then?"

"Again, Brother William will show you the way out."

With that, the furies rained down on us. The sheriff of the county came with an order for us to surrender the tree to his custody. Special notices from the church's solicitors in the city arrived almost once a week by courier, signatures required. One of the nurserymen's lawyers submitted spurious papers asserting that we had reneged on an oral agreement to sell. The district health office asked for inspections for insects and fungi. And the archbishop himself, splendid in folds of magenta, travelled out with his driver in the sleek new Daimler, accompanied by a coterie of young clerics in the jump seats. The great man asked the assembled former brothers to respect the church that had nurtured them for so many years. He threatened that dark prayers could be readily resurrected to punish our disobedience. The world wanted Hyperion, but we did not want to give him up.

Time went on with no success for our adversaries, each of whose forays came to naught. Hyperion continued to thrive on the edge of the glade, now a wide-trunked adult with high spreading branches. The woods surrounding him sprouted with many seedlings, his progeny making a new forest within the forest. Farmer Dockery would, in time, take the trees down, so we were living on borrowed, golden time. The nursery prospered, continuing to sell the other offerings, and our bank account became substantial. Life at the abbey was good.

Despite the offers from Brother William and the others to do so, I took over all the care for and visits to Hyperion, going to him at all hours in all weather. On a sunny spell after several snowstorms, I walked into the glade from the far side, pausing to admire Hyperion from afar. I imagined I could see the glittered eyes of green men and sprites in the verge behind him, watching for whatever was to come. They would take up their rightful ownership when we were gone. Even in dormancy, Hyperion exuded his vigor, with pale, ribbed branches coursing out against the evergreen background. I brought for myself a small lunch of bread and cheese. The snow nearby had melted, so I walked across the open glade to sit down and lean my back against his trunk as I ate. There was what seemed to be the rustle of green men in the dark shadows of the woods, softly talking and laughing, but it might have just been the wind. I put my hand back behind me on the trunk, the gray bark as smooth and pleasing as the skin of a man. With trepidation and guilt, I gave myself to the father of the sun in the pallid winter light, letting the fullness of his power again cascade in strong ripples throughout my body.

YELLOW EYES
IN THE GARDEN

Henry noticed the crow for the first time during his nap on a late winter day. It was warmer than usual; the French doors to his bedroom were open, the air coursing through the house to clean out the musty, closed-up smells. He first saw the crow through the side window, alone on the fence. Then the crow flew down and took a drink out of the stone trough that Henry kept filled for the birds, even in winter. The water often froze solid on cold nights, but not on this day.

Afterwards the crow walked across the terrace in front of the open door, pausing to look in and consider the supine Henry. Almost as if deciding whether or not it was safe to enter the house, the crow looked this way and that in the bedroom. Henry made a clucking sound, the sort he imagined might be pleasant for a bird to hear. The crow made no reaction to the sound, but stood there, looking in.

"Come on in, sweetheart," Henry said, "don't be afraid."

The crow made the slightest movement forward, then, thinking otherwise, backed up and walked away. Henry could hear the flap of wings as it flew off and wondered if it would come back during naptime tomorrow.

It did return, first a moment roosting on the fence, down to the water for a drink, and then across the terrace to the open doors. It looked left and right, as if checking for oncoming traffic and stood there looking up at Henry, who was lying on his side on the bed. This pattern continued for more than a week but stopped for a few days when snow storms returned.

If patient men exist, Henry was one. He had taken the opportunity during the days of falling snow to read about crows on the internet. A solitary crow, he learned, was probably an outcast from the flock, or "murder," as people who like words would say. It would almost certainly be a male and any of his attempts to return to the flock would be met with great noise and pecking. Scientists were unclear as to why single birds were expelled, unless the dominant male in the flock found him a danger to the females. The poor solitary crow must sleep alone in trees away from the communal settling-down of the flock at dark and would be attacked if he came too near them. Crows which are pets could live for thirty years, but crows in the wild have a shorter life span. Folk tales say they can reach centuries of age, but such stories are perhaps only wishful thinking by poets.

Henry thought it was highly unfair the crows would gang up on one of their own and reflected on his place on the periphery of the art community in which he lived. His current paintings did not meld with what recently popular painters were doing, and his pieces were considered both arcane and out-of-date. As a young man his work had sold readily to many collectors, but in time those who liked his canvases either died or moved on to more newly fashionable pieces. He nevertheless painted at the easel every day and his works, both old and new, now crowded the shelves of his studio storage room.

It was obvious to Henry that if the crow did not want to come inside, he himself would have to go outside to have a conversation. Winter turned to spring, and his favorite garden bench in the shade of a crab-apple tree

was the perfect place to wait for the crow. He took Robert Graves's book of Greek myths and sat each afternoon for an hour or two in the shade delving into its pages. In the studio he had been working on a series of landscapes of the Delphic hillsides, steep terraced slopes with red rocks and columnar junipers, and the myths gave him stories to think about as he painted. He imagined that Greek landscapes were better if they were wrapped in the mythological thoughts of the painter, just as the cheese and eggplant gratin would be better when the cook entertained thoughts of summers in Provence. There was no way to test his theory, but Henry was comfortable with it.

The crow looked into the garden several times a day, flying nearby and landing on the parapet of the studio. Not wanting to appear too eager, Henry made no effort to commune as the crow came down to the water bowl. He would let the crow make the first move and this could take a long time. As the weather warmed into summer, the crow continued his daily visits for water and Henry acted as if he had not seen him. They used the garden as if unaware of each other.

Then it occurred to Henry to read the Greek myths aloud. He started over at the beginning with the Prometheus origin myths, intoning across the blooming perennials and ripening rows of vegetables. Neighbors already considered Henry a very strange man, so if they heard his deep voice on a summer zephyr they took no notice. After all, queer artists made queer noises.

When Henry got to the story of Elektra, the crow appeared to pay attention, walking slowly toward the garden bench. Reaching what he considered a safe distance from this man making odd noises, he hopped on a low wall near the bench. For half an hour he slowly rocked his head from side to side as Henry spoke, and the myth came to its end.

Henry reread the Elektra myth the next day, eliciting the exact same reaction from the crow. He continued to recount the travails of the Argos royal family, to the crow's apparent rapt interest, its head moving back and forth as if to music. Henry decided that this was the lure he needed to entice the bird inside, so the following day he returned to his studio to read with the windows and doors wide open. Without hesitation, the crow walked inside and stationed himself on the high back of Henry's daybed. After thirty minutes or so of listening to the doomed family's saga, the crow hopped down and walked quickly out. Day after day Henry's readings were interspersed with his time at the easel as the crow watched. Henry had never been comfortable with anyone else in his studio, but this was different, as there was no need to listen to comments or return pleasantries. The crow was silent but there. He finished his recitation of the entire meltdown of the unhappy Argos family and its emptied throne.

Questions naturally arose in Henry's mind: Did the yellow-eyed crow, in any way, really *understand*? Did the names of Elektra, Orestes, Agamemnon, and the rest bring up a deep-seated familiarity? Where should he go from here? These were minor concerns of Henry's day, however, because his new paintings were going so well. His depictions of Delphi became finer as the myriad details of the thickly treed hillsides emerged. He mixed his colors with ease, odd shades that had an Italianate quality – yellowed hues from the walls of Naples and brownish reds from roof tiles in Tuscany. He even knew without thinking the right shade for a *sfumato* bank of clouds in the distance, and purples mixed with burnt siennas filled in for shadows. He was not sure from where this new dexterity had arisen, but surely it had to be traced to the bird, the only new arrival in his life. He wondered if the crow was five hundred years old, as the legends had it, and had sat on similar daybeds in stone-walled Florentine studios and later in Impressionist Paris.

But Henry thought it only right and proper that he acknowledge the crow's role in his new artistic excellence by including its image. He returned to earlier paintings and placed a small crow, almost hidden, in the terrace shadows or elsewhere. There were ten paintings in the series and the crow could be found somewhere in each of them, often in a difficult-to-find position, not to be quickly perceived. As crows are the archenemies of owls, so beloved of the Greeks, it was an odd image to be included in these classical landscapes.

Pernel O'Brian owned the gallery where Henry used to show his work, before his paintings had stopped selling. O'Brian had been unhappy to dump Henry from his roster of painters, but facts were facts. Gallery wall space was not museum space, he explained. Nonetheless, the two men remained friendly over the years, and O'Brian kept up with Henry through an annual visit to his studio. A full year had passed when he called and asked for a time to visit.

"Good to see you, old friend," Henry said, opening the door to his studio.

"I never tire of the aroma of turpentine, but is there something new about the studio today?" O'Brian's old-fashioned, gentle manners were a delight, as was his very old-fashioned three-piece tweed suit with a gold watch chain across the vest, a guise that told he came from a privileged world. It was correctly assumed he was the scion of a wealthy New England family, too ambitious to remain drinking single malt with his siblings in the evenings of their spacious white-clapboard houses in Braintree. Only a very brave soul would dare ask him for a discount on his artistic wares.

"There *is* something new. See what you find."

O'Brian walked into the large space, now hung with the Delphic paintings on the long walls and the spaces between the windows. The myopic gallery owner wore thick lenses and Henry watched as he walked in and slightly bent to pull tortoise-shell spectacles from his vest pocket. He moved very close to one of the paintings and looked with near-sighted intensity over the surface – up and down, side to side – then stood back for a while. He turned around, walked to the opposite wall and scrutinized the biggest of the paintings, the one with a cadmium sunset raking across the Greek slopes and deep shadows.

"Oh, my gracious, Henry."

He inspected each of the ten works in turn, picking up speed as he went about the room. The last canvas he lightly touched with his forefinger, as if checking a pound cake for doneness.

"Well, we must have an exhibit. I will ask Michael to pick these up tomorrow."

"They need to be framed."

"I think not. The public needs to see these as I have seen them. Unfettered."

"Should we discuss prices?"

"You trusted me to get the optimum price years ago."

"And I still do."

"And, did a new guiding light walk into your life?"

"Perhaps so."

"She must be beautiful beyond measure."

"A yellow-eyed beauty who came into the garden, but now seems to have flown."

"Whom I cannot wait to meet."

O'Brian might not really want to meet, Henry thought, this particular muse. Thus the first new exhibit for Henry Somerset at Fine Arts O'Brian came to be scheduled in record time, the very next month. A woman painter had canceled her showing, nervous about the economy and worried she would have to lower her prices. The new invitations were printed and mailed, bartenders hired for opening night, and cases of white wine put on order. O'Brian kept the paintings hidden away in the back storage room until the actual day of the exhibit.

Henry searched his closet for opening-night dress clothes, long attracting dust at the far back. There was a well-cut black blazer from a London tailor, a black shirt, and matching trousers. No tie was required for the modern world, Henry was happy to learn. His feet had grown a bit wider since he last wore the black loafers (a find at the Ermenegildo Zegna shop in Rome years ago) but they could be shoe-horned on without socks. From superstitions long ago ingrained, he knew not to get a haircut for any new enterprise, so his long face was encircled in an unruly nimbus of white. Altogether, it was not a bad look for an old painter in the twenty-first century.

It could have been an exhibit from forty years ago at Fine Arts O'Brian when the excitement in the room was palpable, people anxious lest someone else buy their heart's desire before they could. The paintings were all sold within the first minutes as attendants hustled to affix the red dots. Henry talked with old faces from years ago, painters he had known back in his palmy days. He joined a group of them near the door, an old-timers' circle reunited.

"What a triumph," a tall woman painter said, hugging him. Local critics often compared her pictures to those of Gainsborough and Sir Joshua Reynolds. But she had also been sidelined by O'Brian's gallery when her beautiful, full-length portraits of English women encased in rich fabrics became difficult to sell.

"I see the Quattrocento everywhere in your paintings," another painter said.

"I haven't thought of you for years. My Becky asked if you were dead," a stocky woman in a floor-length dress said.

"And, Henry, I love, love, love the small image of the crow in each painting," a white-haired man announced. "So inspired."

"I had to include him," Henry said.

"Isn't that a coincidence," the tall woman painter said, "I've befriended a crow in my garden. He watches me paint."

"Did he walk right into your studio?"

"Yes, indeed. And I am embarrassed to say, I have been reading aloud to him. So silly, but I think he really understands Jane Austen. He wiggles his head this way and that as I read. Am I just an old fool?"

"Not at all. There just might be better days coming at the easel, my dear."

PHFFFT

I was packing for the Caribbean cruise, looking forward to a couple of weeks of warm, humid days with my five best friends. We tried to take such a trip every year, to get away from the January cold. The days at sea were always a perfect time to read my current stories and revise them, so I packed a manila folder of the loose pages from my latest work. I could red-pencil them as the pale blue waters glided by or choose to nap in the comfort of the deck chair.

One of the stories was about a woman artist who buys a three-story suburban house with her lottery winnings and invites friends to stay in the many bedrooms. Her neighbors complained to authorities about the recent bohemian night noises. Another piece was about a painter of birds, whose canvases came alive during the night when the birds moved about in the composition. Or did he sleepwalk and repaint them himself? The last was a more personal tale of a man I knew, Robert, who died a few years ago, having never attained the Buddhist enlightenment he so wanted. I had tried to catch the air of excitement he had felt before his last trip to India, ignoring my own skepticism about its outcome. There were only several pages, but they showed promise and a suggestion of the next direction to be taken.

><

Listening to the final movement of Mozart's *Jupiter* Symphony, I felt a sublime and ethereal sadness, my tears welling up at midday. There was a mixture of joy and exaltation in the underlying disharmonies, surely a clarion of paradise. Bright yellow, C Major, but there was also an admixture of darker colors within the forthright chords. It brought to mind another time when Robert was in India, hoping to start the *ngöndro* sessions of a million prostrations and thus open up and cleanse himself. But first he had to deal with life and death matters at the monastery, where testy human concerns often eclipsed the grand search for light.

I wondered if I had been thinking too much about Robert and his beloved Rinpoche, who was suffering from a deadly flowering tumor inside his brain that he appeared to take no action against. All of the disciples knew that their leader could cure himself, if only he would. Since he had already manifested the power to stop blood rushing from a cut or see into other men's thoughts or hold his breath for an hour, why not exercise this simple act of self-survival? He must have known that the end was near and that his inaction was causing a storm at the monastery. His followers ran in circles of despair, a beehive without order or pattern. Robert himself was thrown into a high gear of worry and frustration. I could hear this in his voice when he called me collect on a crackly line from the pay phone in the valley village near the monastery.

"He won't listen. Why doesn't he cure himself?"

"I don't know, Robert. He must have a reason."

"And why doesn't he take a rainbow death? Like the lama in the next valley?"

"Maybe he's waiting for something better."

"That must be it. I will watch for the signs."

We talked along in this manner, Robert full of questions about death and I responding as best an atheist could. A few calls earlier Robert had related with awe the story of the rainbow death in the next valley. An old lama had walked up alone to a windowless mountain hut. All of his followers camped below in the valley, waiting weeks for something to happen. A sudden rainbow across the clear sky was the signal they both dreaded and hoped for. The weeping followers jostled one another as they raced uphill to reach the hut. Inside, the Rinpoche's robes were neatly folded in a corner with only a small pile of fingernails and toenails remaining in the room's center. The unknowable power of the rainbow had presumably taken up the rest. I asked Robert if he had been in the group jostling up to the hut, it being so much a thing he would have done.

"No, no ... but it was in the very next valley over, not ten miles away."

"Did you hear this from someone who was there?"

"Others here in the monastery have. Everybody is talking about it."

"It's a beautiful story, Robert."

"I know you don't believe it, but it really happened."

There were also reports that a very old and venerated Rinpoche several valleys beyond, fifty miles to the east, sensing his own departure, had generated a double rainbow with intense colors in a cloudless sky and left nothing behind. Neither robes nor fingernails were found, every part of him gone. What did I think of that?

"Death never comes the convenient, expected way, Robert. I'm sorry you are so unhappy about your Rinpoche," I said.

The fragility of the telephone connection, with its short gaps and scratchy sound, dissuaded me from expressing my true opinion about these events. I felt guilty for not speaking my mind, as my iconoclastic views of spiritual matters were absolutely clear to me. Robert said he would call again soon.

The blooming tumor grew and took away the Rinpoche, whose death turned out to be just like that of an ordinary person. I could hear Robert's disappointment when he called me.

"He's gone. We had the funeral pyre last week. It lasted all day."

"I'm so sorry, Robert."

"I sent you a small clay votive. They said it would take a month to get there."

"I will keep a lookout for it."

"Rinpoche's ashes are mixed into the clay, so keep it safe."

"I will put it on the shelf next to the Burmese Buddha."

"And please do not write one of your cynical stories about this. Sacred things do not like being written about."

"You know that I can't promise."

Why did such mysterious happenings occur only in the rumpled foothills of the Himalayas? The dry mountain air around me in the west seemed so very different from the vaporous air around Robert, which in my mind's eye was swirling in dense coils of saffron, the very color of the Tibetan lama's robes. It was air that choked the mind, making logical progression of thoughts impossible. Perhaps in such an atmosphere I could come to believe, taken up in the magic nights with butter lamps and echoes of deep-throated horns. We had talked about my joining him in India later that year, but I knew he did not want my secular eyes inspecting his monastery. The trip did not happen.

I again started the last movement of the Mozart, hoping that this miraculous music from another continent and time would instruct me in heavenly happenings here in the west. While listening I was sure that I could hear as well as see color in the music: I heard a distinct narrow line of maroon embellishments amid the upward crush of violins, coiling in and around the arpeggios. Had I at last given in to the power of suggestion?

><

That is as far as I got with my story. One morning on the cruise ship, we were all beside each other in six shaded lounge chairs on the ship's pool deck. The others were reading, listening to earphones full of opera or picking up messages on their mobile phones. I got out my dog-eared manila folder, hoping that a conclusion to the story might materialize. The Rinpoche pages brought nothing to mind. I decided to work later on the more accessible stories, putting the open folder beside me on the adjoining chair, with the red pencil to weigh down its pages.

Perhaps a swim in the cool pool on the center deck would stimulate my brain, making the writing easier. It was a still day on deck, although we were sailing north at a reported fifteen knots, with a bright sun. Only the occasional light breeze rippled across our chairs, lifting the edges of the towels.

The pool water was refreshing and a dozen laps sufficed for my cooling.

As I sat down again in the deck chair, I was too wet to resume work. I thought I heard a "phffft" sound as I closed my eyes and lay back to dry off. It did not hold my attention at the time as cruise ships make many odd noises, even on the smooth sea days. I would return to the editing later. Conversation kept us all busy for half an hour as we laughed at recent Panamanian adventures ashore.

I picked up the folder again. The Rinpoche story was not there, although all the others were, as well as the red pencil. There was nothing to be found when I searched behind me on the deck for white, strewn-about manuscript pages. No culprit appeared to have crumpled them away in his beach bag, and the sea was like glass as I looked out, wondering.

The remainder of the morning remained cloudless and the windward islands of Belize slipped by on the horizon, green and inviting. We walked up the steps to the Lido Cafe for a late lunch, where I told the others about my missing story. Discussing it, we came to the only logical conclusion – that an errant wisp of wind had picked up the pages and sent them fluttering over the railing to the uttermost parts of the sea. The consensus was against any supernatural hand having a part in the disappearance, in favor of a mere aerodynamic oddity, even though doubt still lingered in my mind about how a wind had such dexterity. My friends were sensible to the one. Conversation drifted off to lesser matters, whether the tuna melt sandwich was better than the chicken tandoori. I could not help but wonder if it was the ship's engine

vibrations that made the expanding concentric rings on my saffron-hued lobster bisque while the thin drizzled circle of red pepper sauce grew larger, as if upwelling straight towards me from the ocean floor.

THE
FOUR-HUNDRED-YEAR
FANFARE

The ad in the local newspaper said it all.

Call for Sample Entries

The Committee of Four Hundred Years
will award a commission for a fanfare
of not more than three minutes' duration
to celebrate Santa Fe's Quadricentennial.
Please submit a score and/or a recording
with your actual fanfare for the judges.
Commission honorarium is $10,000.
New Mexico residents only
with minority composers given preference.

The paper was delivered to the outlying pueblos in the early morning, most often thrown on the front yards or portals of the adobe houses. Charles Setting Sun lived alone in one of these houses, assigned to him by the council a few years ago. At age twenty-seven, he had returned to his pueblo after a decade of music study in New York, having been awarded a full Juilliard scholarship on the basis of his high school composition for string quartet, coupled with his impeccable minority status. His professors and coaches had been awed by the ability of this boy from Indian country. How had such sophisticated expertise arisen, from the outset so much greater than that of his fellow students?

Holiday trips to the pueblo from New York were out of the question because of Charles's limited resources. The Juilliard dormitory was housed on the upper floors of a building in the Lincoln Center Complex. His room had a view of the East River, and it was a subject of jokes among his fellow students that Charles Setting Sun saw only the rising sun. He spent his Christmas, Easter, summer, and Thanksgiving holidays in the city, walking from museum to museum and going to concerts, as his memories of the pueblo grew fainter. Now alone after his parents' deaths, he wrote only occasionally to his beloved auntie back home.

His principal professor was Julianna Grabowski, the only woman and the tallest among the composition faculty. Just to look at her invoked fear in a first-year student. Her dark eyes could settle upon you, dissolve you into a whimpering, self-doubting puddle. However, she adored Setting Sun from the beginning, recognizing a fellow tall outcast with a past that mirrored hers, with its out-of-favor Polish bloodlines. She nurtured, polished, and challenged him, listening as his compositions grew in brilliance and complexity. She felt he would be the composer of his generation, melding the natural sounds and native music of his childhood with the learned traditions of Europe. A great future awaited when the right road opened up for him.

"You must be prepared," she said, "for a life of penury. Despite your great promise, few composers make a living from commissions."

"I think I might," Charles answered.

"If anyone can, my dear, you just might."

Because of the economic downturn, graduation came and went with no offers to Charles for further academic study, no roads to the tops of the mountains. Grabowski advised him to be patient and agree to nothing that could conflict with a future university offer. She would visit him, she promised. He packed up his compositions in a carrying case and returned by transcontinental bus to his tribal home in New Mexico.

The council fathers were in a quandary about their talented son. They had received reports on his progress at Juilliard and were proud of his extraordinary ability, but did not understand it nor know how they could find the proper place for him in the community. If Charles had been a painter or a potter, there would have been an immediate opening for him in one of numerous studios. A many-faceted composer fit into none of their round holes.

Perhaps it was the quiet influence of the matriarchs, who held no official power in the council, that determined its decision. The council voted to give Charles a house, a secondhand grand piano, and a small monthly stipend to pursue his compositions. Music was just as important as painting, the women had argued, and the pueblo should provide for all its members, no matter their differences.

Charles was unusual in other ways. He was thin, tall, long-fingered, and high-voiced, unlike the strong and stout pueblo men. From early on he was smarter than the other boys. He could run like a white-tailed deer, but more popular, rough-and-tumble sports were not for him. He was not teased or bullied, but given special respect, like a stalk of corn that grows much taller than the rest. The mothers said that maybe the future of the pueblo might lie in his hands: his unusual powers could prove useful in future eras of discord.

He had been happy in New York, with its egalitarian musical society, one largely based upon merit and accomplishment. Matters of lineage, matriarchs, and clan connection were irrelevant there. His peers at school looked at the man, the composer and his compositions, rather than his antecedents.   His master's project, a concerto for two cellos and string quartet, brought down the house as he played one of the cellos, his adoring Dr. Grabowski the other.

For two years after his return from New York, the whole pueblo heard at one time or another piano music emanating from his adobe house, often late into the night. Sometimes a single tune, one note at a time, and other times crashing, painful chords. When he read the Four-Hundred-Year Steering Committee's ad in the paper, he knew that this was his opportunity.

The economy was still fragile on his return. How had Santa Fe come up with such a prize when the city budget was in ruins? One of the members of the committee, a single woman named Annis McCord, had a notable trust fund, proposed the fanfares idea, and offered to donate the prize. She was worried about the pennypinching plans that the steering committee had proposed – speeches on the plaza by the mayor and some state senators. There were no provisions for rental chairs, robes, banners, finery or airline tickets for the invited Spanish nobility.

McCord felt this would not do. Several years earlier when she had been at the Chartres Cathedral on Armistice Day, she marveled as the west doors of the nave were opened for the procession of the fragile, Great War veterans. Fanfares of trumpets, French horns, and drums accompanied the stiff-backed old men as they marched into the cathedral at sunset. What a stunning mix, she thought, as golden light and music soared through the doors, bestowing honor and glory on the old warriors. Maybe an original group of fanfares, resounding throughout Santa Fe, would bring similar joy and luster to the city. Why had she been left a fortune from her family's New England ball-bearing factory except to help others and embellish their lives? McCord almost could hear the majesty of the fanfares in her mind and knew that this was why her grandmother had bequeathed her the house on the hill and so much money.

Little did she know that the majesty was being composed in the small pueblo house, one note at a time. Charles intended to make a recording of his finished fanfares as his competitive entry. He drove to the Santa Fe southside row of pawn shops and bought a trumpet, a cornet, a large drum, and a French horn, all for two hundred dollars. The tarnished dents would make no difference in the sound. These purchases, including a small high-fidelity recorder, required him to request a small monetary advance from the council.

A degree in composition from Juilliard entailed acquiring knowledge of many musical instruments and how they blended together in a symphony orchestra. Charles was an adequate trumpet and cornet soloist, and the French horn had always been one of his favorites. His facility with drums came almost as a pueblo birthright.

He performed the first fanfare on a single trumpet, starting with slow notes in a rising scale, coming back on itself, then rising higher and higher, softer for a while, ending with a final arpeggio. On playing back the recording, he realized another voice was needed, so he recorded the mellower cornet part over the trumpet. This time the notes circled around the prior notes, coming to a dissonant meeting, resolving and then rising above the main melody in a double-fast shadow. The two melodies met in the final notes, equals at last. He thought of morning glories that often circled around the corn.

In a flush of excitement, he worked into the morning hours. The last and fifth fanfare was for a single cornet, seven trumpets, and three French horns. It was slower, truly the most majestic of the five, with the first notes rising together in a trial flight like the cranes he saw along the river, fluttering in low circles. Then the trumpets led the way to the finale, the French horns adding a fullness, to a climax of twelve splendid chords, their complexity progressing in a stately march with the final statement made by the sweet tone of a single cornet. Would the judges notice the classical quotations in his work, especially the bits from Old Spain? In his mind's eye he could see his fanfares being played by a group marching into the east gate of the Alhambra, with snow still on the mountains, stiff white ruffs on all the players.

Nobody in that part of the pueblo slept well that night as the grandiosity filled their ears. Neighbors knew their musical son had opened a new chapter when he played his compositions at full volume again and again. They suspected that something fine and good had been born that night in Charles's adobe house. Several listening women worried about his solitary life, deciding to bring him casseroles more often.

He took his recording the next morning to the committee offices in Santa Fe to fill out the submission form at the secretary's desk. She was an older woman with a large bun of very black hair. He had to push back the alabaster-engraved name sign, *Mrs. Rodriguez*, and the pot of struggling philodendron to find a flat surface on which to write.

"You're not the first, you know," Mrs. Rodriguez said as he wrote. "We've had three entries already."

"It's only been three days since the ad."

"I know. You composers are a quick-working lot."

Charles gave her his completed form, which she read slowly while adjusting her glasses, asking several questions about his handwriting. She said that he also was not the first minority to enter.

"Who else?"

"Hispanics are considered minorities, even with so many of us in Santa Fe. There are two of them, and the third is an Anglo, a short red-headed man, not a minority. His name was odd enough to be a minority, though. Meadowlark Philpott."

"I wonder how many entries there will be."

"We hope for a lot. By the way, my sister's daughter married one of you pueblo people."

"Which pueblo?"

"I can't remember the new native name, but it's next to the bridge on the Rio Grande. They go to all the festivals, but she's not allowed to dance. There's a ten-dollar fee, please."

As he drove along the river back to his house, Charles was depressed. He was sure that the award would be based upon minority status rather than quality of the fanfares. What did music have to do with political castes? His confidence sank as he thought how different the audience here would be from the appreciative ears at Juilliard.

His auntie came by the next morning with a jar of apricot jam made from the fruit of the big tree in the pueblo plaza. "This is for my lamb. To wash away the clouds."

"I don't know if my fanfares will win, but they are good, Auntie."

"Everything you do is good and full of beauty," Auntie said. "You shouldn't worry."

Auntie was small and round. He remembered as a boy wanting to be short like her and her brothers, to fit in with the other pueblo people. But she always said that he was tall because the river willows made music in the wind. No songs came from the boulders.

Time passed slowly for Charles in the weeks before the announcement of the competition's winner. He knew that exercise was a good leveler of bad spirits, so he took to running around the pueblo. He ran across the plaza to the white cliffs, then along the river until the path cut across to the other side. His long legs, so difficult to find pants for, propelled him with the long stride he had used every morning in New York. Even in the summer beauty of the land, with the fullness of the pathside grasses and leaves, he could not keep his mind off the competition.

In the quiet pueblo night, an idea took full form in Charles's mind. With the first rays of sun over the mountains, he ruffled though the pages of the Santa Fe telephone directory. And there it was – *Philpott, M. 18 Quintana Lane. 545-9921.*

All the good composers back at school got up early, so an early call would be the first test. The man passed handily with a cheery, "Meadowlark here."

"This is Charles Setting Sun. May I come by and hear your fanfares?"

"Fanfare, single, Charles. I just did one."

"Is now too early?"

"Not at all. I'll put a new pot of coffee on."

"Twenty-five minutes."

Slipping a copy of his fanfare into his jacket pocket, he raced into Santa Fe before the morning rush, sun visor down against the bright sun. He remembered Quintana Lane, right behind Cristo Rey Church, from his year in the boys' choir there. He wondered if Meadowlark had been in a choir as he knocked on the door of the small adobe, which appeared to be a single room from the outside.

"Come in, Charles." If people called Charles willowy, Meadowlark could have earned a title of oaken. He was solid, rooted, of-the-earth as much as Charles was of sky and clouds – five-foot seven to Charles's six-foot four. They were bound to become friends by all laws of magnetism and opposite energy.

"Did you sing the Brahms *Requiem* as a boy?" Charles asked.

"I still remember the words. *Selig sind, die da Leid tragen*. Blessed are they that mourn," Meadowlark said, pouring two mugs of coffee. "I don't remember any other German, though."

"I knew it. One of us is going to win."

"You don't need to hear my fanfare?"

"Not really. But let's listen."

Meadowlark's music was quite different from Charles's. Rather than starting off with trumpets, he started with French horns. Odd chords splayed out between the horns, soft and dissonant, then coming together in a single note. Then many trumpets played above the other instruments, almost hurting the ears with their widely spread notes. The jarring notes slowly vanished, one at a time, until the whole ensemble played four triumphant chords, one after the other. Out of a many-voiced disorder came order, and immense, elegant beauty.

"It's even better than I imagined," Charles said. "You'll win."

Meadowlark had passed all the tests Charles had outlined in his head. First, there was a certain queerness that all true composers possessed, a way of breaking the rules, a way of then following them, an elegance of movement, and finally, the element of surprise. He had all of these. And for Charles there was a definite sexiness in Meadowlark's red hair and solidness, as if he were a forbidden cousin in this new family of music. He almost smiled as he thought about himself and this Anglo man being attracted to each other, because he was sure there was a return of his regard. Nobody in his twenty-some years had ever given him such a look.

"Let's hear yours," Meadowlark said.

Charles played the entire recording. He listened to his own music with a disinterested ear, as had his professors back at Juilliard. It was good. Maybe he and Meadowlark were a match. He did not know which of the entries would win.

There was a long silence before Meadowlark responded. "I would be at loggerheads to make a choice. If the competition is one to ten, we're both at nine point seven seven seven." Meadowlark had in his mind a process similar to Charles's, now giving him top grades. There was also something definitely arousing about this pueblo man's lankiness and his odd aroma. He wanted to spend more time with this new friend, who also seemed interested in more than his music.

"Do you think we could work together? Write a fanfare between us?" Meadowlark asked.

"I never have had luck at composing with somebody else." Charles remembered several unfortunate nights with fellow-students, usually women who wanted to make other than heavenly arias.

"Want to give it a try, anyway?"

It was the voice from Charles's dark inside rooms that answered, not the voice from the light-filled, logical, and music-oriented plateaus of the mind. "Let's do."

That was the start of a long day. Meadowlark had all the same collection of dented and unpolished instruments that he had found in the local pawnshops. Turning on his recorder, he started with a trumpet, playing a slow arpeggio that he thought Charles would like. Charles did and played it back to him on another trumpet. They played in unison again and once again. Then Charles played a round of a few notes later while Meadowlark played the theme. From there the fanfare grew like a summer vine, clambering over itself and doubling back again. They brought in the cornets and the French horns, getting more excited as the sun rose high above Santa Fe's east side. By late afternoon they had it, a fanfare that they both knew used the best voices from each of their other pieces, melding them into a splendid new whole. They had been able to work as a team, to compose with two voices that variously supported, then surmounted, then hid away in dissonance and finally came together into a singleness. It was better than what each had done on his own.

"Now *that's* a fanfare," Meadowlark said while he wrote down the notes on a blank musical page.

"Let's go see Mrs. Rodriguez. We can use our middle names."

She was just about to close for the day, packing the hand-lotion bottle, cell-phone, glasses, and paperback novel into her handbag. It had been church-mouse quiet all day, so why was there a knock in the last three minutes?

"Oh, it's you two."

"We have another fanfare for you," Charles said.

"From a very good friend, named Borden McNess," Meadowlark said.

"Is that a minority name?"

"Half so. Half Pueblo and half honky."

"We don't find humor in the plight of minorities."

"Neither do we. Half minority is as good as full minority."

"Ten dollars."

She put the two fives into the file folder and stood up to go.

"Is Borden a man or a woman?"

"Does it matter?" Meadowlark asked.

"No. Let's wish him or her good luck."

And their fanfare won the prize: a ten-thousand-dollar check and the critic's choice award. Borden McNess, of course, could not be found for the award ceremonies so the two men sat in for their friend. They met the two pale-skinned but still vital Spanish contessas who had come for the event and were much taken up by the music of the new world. Annis McCord thought the winning piece was oddly familiar, but she could not identify why.

Mrs. Rodriguez asked the two men, officially McNess's friends, to give McNess the check and the

Nambé-ware platter in the shape of a flattened zucchini, on which McNess's name was misspelled in etched block letters. After opening a checking account at the Great River National Bank in the name of Borden McNess, with Charles and Meadowlark as co-signers, that should have been the end of the masquerade. They would move on, feeling a bit flusher, more successful, and happy, each with a newfound friend and a secret to share.

That whole summer, the McNess fanfare was heard at odd times throughout the city, echoing down Burro Alley and against the basilica walls. It was played from the roof of the Audubon Center at noon, filling the entire valley. The circular balcony of the state capitol building was a favorite place for the musicians, trumpets resounding in the hallways. Brass sections of school bands were assigned to play the fanfare at sunset on the plaza, a different school chosen each week. Meadowlark thought he heard somebody in the supermarket checkout line humming it. Santa Fe's anniversary summer resounded with brassy joy, thanks to Annis McCord.

But she had sensed something was amiss. She thought her ten-thousand-dollar donation entitled her to know more about the shadowy but gifted winning composer. She invited Charles and Meadowlark to her hillside house for lunch, the next best thing to having McNess. They seemed such an odd pair, this very tall, poetic Pueblo man and this stocky Scotsman or Irishman or whatever. A keen reader of detective stories, Annis vowed to herself to use the luncheon to get to the bottom of this matter. Something smelled wrong. The two contessas, still in town for a week or so, were included to provide witnesses amid the chicken salad and chilled white wine.

When all were seated and the luncheon well underway, Annis said, "It has been a glorious summer, don't you think? The McNess fanfare has given all of Santa Fe a lift."

The taller of the two contessas said, "We hear a note of Southern Spain in it, don't we, Altessa?"

"Indeed," she said, "it rings of home."

Charles resisted saying thank you. He worried that their deception would in time be revealed. "A wonderful composer," Annis said, "but we don't know whether this Borden McNess is a man or a woman. Which is it?"

Meadowlark answered, "We promised not to tell."

"Such loyalty..." Annis said. "Well I have a scheme to flush out the truth. I will commission the composer for a string quartet for next year's Chamber Music Festival. He or she will come out of the dark, like a bluebird coming to a replenished feeder. Let's say another ten thousand dollars."

"What if Borden McNess is not a single person at all, but something else?" Meadowlark asked.

"What else? An amazing poodle or a very talented canary?"

"Something else. Would it also get the ten thousand dollars?"

"I have to admit I'm intrigued. Yes, I think so, but I would first have to approve the submitted string quartet."

Thus the composing career of Borden McNess took off in a slow but steady ascent. Annis McCord and the chamber music directors were delighted with the quartet, which brought resounding acclaim during the following festival season. Another commission resulted for the next season, this time for a chamber concerto for oboe and cello. Another ten thousand dollars. An octet the next season. Twenty thousand dollars. A concerto for piano and chamber ensemble for the season after that. Also twenty thousand dollars. Annis thought with amusement that while the family ball bearings had rolled American industry forward in the last century, she now used them to smooth the unfolding of serious modern music.

People booked in advance for the front seats at a new McNess commission, and orchestras around the world were requesting performance rights. In the small world of serious music, the McNess name began to glow. I Musici included McNess pieces in a concert at the elegant town hall in Perugia. The chamber ensemble from the Berlin Symphony scheduled two McNess pieces for an all-modern evening, while the music festival at Donaueschingen requested to play the now admired Opus Four Octet.

It was rumored that McNess might well be a cloistered nun, by her vows required to remain anonymous; or a blind man, preferring to stay in his musical darkness; or the husband of a privacy-seeking political leader. And just this year, it was passed around that McNess was the clairvoyant widow of a long-dead composer who had summoned his notes from the netherworld. After eight years, only Charles and Meadowlark knew the truth, not even their now long-time friend and supporter, Annis McCord.

Since nobody had heard of two people who wrote music together, there was no suspicion that such a thing could be. Composers were by nature solitary beings with strong egos. Annis, thinking of the Grimm brothers, once asked if McNess were kept chained by an overlord in some dungeon, hoping a new composition would result in freedom.

It was another summer and Annis was hosting a luncheon to celebrate the premiere of the latest piece from McNess, this one a well-received monodrama for a full-bodied woman's voice and piano quartet, the libretto a story by an obscure local author. Charles and Meadowlark were invited, as well as professor Grabowski, who now spent summers at Annis's big house on the hill, the two woman having bonded at an earlier festival concert. The McCord millions had found a nonmusical road to travel, nurturing happiness like an August rainstorm on a parched garden.

The two contessas, reliable fixtures now at summer Santa Fe music events, still walked on their own with

parasols up the hill to the McCord house. They had been included since the McNess compositions began and considered themselves part of the founding cabal. It had become their pattern to discuss the new commission among the six of them as they picked over their cold luncheon, munching cheese sticks and drinking white wine. Without admitting it in words, they knew in their hearts that the McCord terrace table was a cutting edge of modern music. What was decided there would contribute over and over to the livelihood of orchestras and chamber groups around the world.

"Dearest Annis, I never grow weary of your chicken-salad lunches," the tall contessa said.

"Cook would be unhappy if we had anything else," Annis replied, wondering if truth ever came out of those Spanish lips.

"My sister and I just came from the open rehearsal for the Brahms Sextet. Superb. Superb."

"That sextet is so difficult," Grabowski said, standing

behind Annis's chair. "My students all want to play it, but I parcel it out to only the most gifted."

"Two violins, two cellos, and two violas." The contessa adjusted her comb with an all-knowing look and speared a morsel of mayonnaise-covered chicken.

"Let's ask McNess for the same next summer. A sextet for violins, cellos, and violas," Annis said.

"It will be hard competing with the Brahms," Grabowski said. "What do you think, Charles and Meadowlark? Is your McNess up to it?"

"I am sure McNess is up to it," Meadowlark answered, avoiding the personal pronoun lest it reveal their secret.

"You seem awfully sure of your friend," Annis said.

"Borden McNess won't let us down."

Charles wondered if Grabowski knew the real truth. She must have heard the pueblo influences in the many summers of new compositions, but he admired her for keeping her counsel to herself.

Both Annis and Grabowski had noticed, Charles was sure, when he let his hand linger on his lover's forearm. Would the story ever be told of what a joy it was for the two men to work together, blending their music again and again? They knew that the sum of their two parts grew to a thing far better than what they started with. It was a secret that supported their love.

Charles smiled what he thought was an assenting smile. Their joint account at the Great River National Bank had continued to grow, not only with the commission money from Annis McCord, but from the new fees generated from the many performances across the musical world. Checks arrived denominated in Euros, Swiss francs, British pounds and, the last deposit, Singapore dollars. Charles had been able to buy a new stove and other gifts for his Auntie, and the council now received a regular repayment. Meadowlark often sent several checks home to his Indiana parents.

Their days were taken up with music, one often playing for the other a new composition that had sprung up in the night. They talked about what would happen at the disclosure of their subterfuge, would it become music by Setting Sun and Philpott or the other way around? They talked about the lack of ego required to be a composing pair, each savoring the other's strengths.

Composing time was treated as a treasure, Charles staying overnight at Meadowlark's adobe until a new work was near completion. Meadowlark also spent nights at the pueblo house, as their time there was more sensual and satisfying when accompanied by the sound of the river as they made love. Neighbors saw the two walking along the riverbank at sunrise, laughing as they skimmed rocks across the surface or climbed on the rocks for a better view. When they drove together into the countryside around the pueblo, at times Charles sensed a third person behind them in the rear seat, listening to their talk.

CPSIA information can be obtained
at www.ICGtesting.com
Printed in the USA
FSHW020948080819
60840FS